Bones in the basket

For my dad

Other books by C.J. Taylor:

How Two-Feather was saved from loneliness
The Ghost and Lone Warrior
Little Water and the gift of the animals
The secret of the white buffalo
How we saw the world: Nine Native stories of the way things began
The monster from the swamp: Native legends of monsters, demons, and other creatures
The Messenger of Spring

Published in Canada by Tundra Books, *McClelland & Stewart Young Readers,*
481 University Avenue, Toronto, Ontario M5G 2E9

Published in the United States by Tundra Books of Northern New York,
P.O. Box 1030, Plattsburgh, New York 12901

Library of Congress Catalog Number: 94-61786

Also available in a French edition, ***Des os dans un panier: Légendes amérindiennes sur les origines du monde***, ISBN 0-88776-344-8

Canadian Cataloguing in Publication Data

Taylor, C.J. (Carrie J.), 1952-
    Bones in the basket : Native stories of the origin of people

ISBN 0-88776-327-8 (bound)   ISBN 0-88776-450-9 (pbk.)

1. Indians of North America – Folklore.   2. Creation – Folklore.
3. Legends – North America.   I. Title.

PS8589.A88173B65 1998   j398.2'097'0708997   C97-932766-0
PZ8.1.T39B64 1998

We acknowledge the support of the Canada Council for the Arts for our publishing program.

Design by Michael Dias

Printed in Hong Kong by South China Printing Co. Ltd.

Sources

Blanchard, David, *Seven Generations: A History of the Kanienkehaka,* Kahnawake, QC:
    Kahnawake Survival School, 1980.
Burland, Cottie, *North American Indian Mythology*, New York: Peter Bedrick Books, 1991.
Erdoes, Richard and Ortiz, Alfonso, eds., *American Indian Myths and Legends,*
    New York: Pantheon Books, 1984.
Liebert, Robert M., *Osage Life and Legends*, Happy Camp, CA: Naturegraph Publishers, Inc., 1987.
Norman, Howard, ed., *Northern Tales: Traditional Stories of Eskimo and Indian People,*
    New York: Pantheon Books, 1990.
Spence, Lewis, *Myths and Legends: North American Indians*, London: Studio Editions, 1993.

Some of the designs used in this book are inspired by drawings found in *American Indian Design & Decoration* by LeRoy H. Appleton, published by Dover Publications Inc., New York.

2 3 4 5 6   02 01 00 99 98   1 2 3 4 5 6   03 02 01 00 99 98

Bones in the basket
Native stories of the origin of people

C.J.Taylor

Tundra Books

The legends

Introduction

Dear Reader,

There are probably as many different stories of how the earth was formed and how humankind came to inhabit it as there are Native peoples in North America. Different as those legends are, a common thread runs through them. All see the earth as a gift given us, prepared for us ahead of our arrival. All recognize the interdependence of all life on our planet and the obligation to protect it.

Each legend stands on its own. We see how the balance between land and water is achieved, how plant and animal life is provided and the many ways people arrive. They arrive as eagles from worlds above or climb vines from the underworld to reach light. They are formed from the dust of the earth or from dry bones that come alive to natural beauty. Sky and earth unite to parent the first child. Spirits search the heavens for souls and bodies so they might have children and a place for them to live. Twin brothers fight to see whether good or evil will prevail. And Creator, his work accomplished, returns to the heavens to observe how we manage his creation.

These stories inspired me and opened my eyes to the wonders around us. I hope they do the same for you.

Nia wen.

C.J. Taylor

Before all things began

Before all things began there was only "the One that is everything" — the Creator. All else was nothing. All else was blackness. The Creator created life from his own being.

First he caused great mists to rise. From these mists, he pulled light out and created the sun.

The sun shone brightly and melted the mists so that rain fell. The rain gathered and grew into a large sea. The Creator gave life to the water. The sun warmed it so that land appeared.

The Creator then separated Father Sky from Mother Earth and gave them the form of a man and a woman. They came together to give birth to humankind. But before the first child could be born, the earth had to be prepared for its arrival.

Mother Earth took a bowl of water and showed how mountains should grow to separate the land. She then stirred the water into a foam that rose and became a rainbow, then clouds.

Father Sky blew on the clouds and rain fell, making the ground fertile. He took grains of corn in his hand and placed them in the sky as stars to brighten the night. He then gave Mother Earth other grains of corn to plant in the fertile ground so that their children would always have food.

The birth of the first child could now take place.

From darkness to light

Below the earth, there was another world. It was a dreary place, always cold and dark. The people of that world were not happy. They wished to have light and warmth. They sent out scouts to find a better place to live.

One day the scouts returned with good news. They had found a new world. It was like nothing anyone had ever seen: a world where the sun shone and the waters ran clear, a place with game to hunt and food to gather.

The people readied themselves to journey to this new world. They followed the scouts for many days through the darkness of the underworld until they came to a place where they saw a faint light. A vine root hung down from the light. A scout led the way and the people climbed up the vine. One by one, they came through the hole into the light and walked upon the earth for the first time.

They raised their faces to the warm sun. They felt the cooling breeze. They smelled the fresh air. They saw before them open plains with herds of game, clear waters full of fish, and mountains with trees and vines heavy with fruit.

Everyone wanted to climb to the beautiful new world. But when only half the people below had reached it, the vine broke. In their impatience to reach the earth above, so many had pulled on the vine at once that it weakened and gave way. The hole closed over.

The people left in the world below still search for a way out of the darkness.

The raft

What should the earth be like? Should it be all water or all land?

Wisagatcak who was a creator wanted land. Giant Beaver who was also a creator wanted water. The two were always fighting.

Wisagatcak decided to get rid of Giant Beaver once and for all. He built a dam as a trap. Then he waited with his spear ready to kill Giant Beaver as he swam in the dammed-up water. But just as he was about to throw his spear, the dam broke and water poured out everywhere. The water flowed and went on flowing out.

Now it was Giant Beaver's turn to work his magic against Wisagatcak. Giant Beaver began to chant and his songs made the waters flow even faster. Soon water was spreading over all the land.

As Wisagatcak saw the water rising, he quickly pulled up some trees and made a raft. On it he rescued animals who were swimming desperately in the water. When all the land was covered with water, Giant Beaver went back to his home, thinking he had won the fight.

But Wisagatcak still had some magic left. Only he needed help. He called on Wolf and gave him a piece of moss that clung to one of the trees. Wolf took the moss in his mouth and ran around the raft in circles. Wherever bits of moss fell, first on the raft and then on the water, earth formed. The earth grew until once again, there was land to share the planet with the water.

Both creators had shown their magic and the limits of their magic. They decided to make peace so that the creatures who lived in water and those that lived on land could exist together.

Big Raven creates the world

Big Raven set out one day to create the world.

He traveled east, west, north and south in search of all the sources of light to ask for advice. He asked Dawn and Sunset, Midday and Midnight. But none gave him any help.

At last he came to a place where the sky and ground come together, the horizon. There he saw a tent. He flew down and looked inside. A group of men were gathered in discussion.

One heard the sound of Big Raven's wings and stepped outside to see what was there.

"Who are you and what do you want?" the man asked.

"I am Big Raven, the creator. Who are you?"

"I am a man. We men were created from the dust that arose when the sky and ground met," explained the man. "We're stuck in this in-between place with nowhere to go. We need a place to live."

"That is what I want to give you, a place to live," said Big Raven. "Come with me and tell me what you need."

Big Raven took the man on his back and they flew off on their search.

The man saw an empty space below. "Look. There!" he called to Big Raven.

Big Raven pulled out feathers and dropped them. As they floated down into the empty space, they formed continents. "But there are no rivers, or mountains, or lakes," the man complained. Big Raven pulled out more feathers. As they floated to the land below, rivers started to flow, mountains rose and trees grew.

The man looked at the beautiful land Big Raven had created and he liked it. "But what will we eat?" he asked.

Big Raven swooped down onto the mountains and gathered chips of wood from the many kinds of trees. He threw the chips into the wind. As they landed, they changed. Those that fell on the land became caribou, bear and fox. Those that dropped on the waters became seals, walrus and fish. Those that floated in the air became birds.

"There. You now have everything," Big Raven said.

The man went back to join the other men. They got busy. They made houses from the trees; they made clothing from the animal skins; they hunted and fished and gathered berries to eat. But something was missing.

They sent the man back to Big Raven.

"We need something else," the man said. "Companions."

"But you have each other," said Big Raven, "and all the animals and birds as your companions."

"It's not enough," the man said. "I need someone like myself and yet not quite like myself. Someone who can give birth to others to continue living here after we have gone. Someone to share the work and care for the new people."

"I don't know if I can make such a companion," Big Raven said. He perched on a rock under a tree to think how it might be done. As if in answer to his thoughts, Spider Woman appeared, hanging and swaying on a thin thread in front of his eyes.

"I can help you," she said. "Watch." She started to spin a web and the first woman appeared. The man rushed to embrace her. His last need was fulfilled.

Spider Woman went on spinning women for the men. Together men and women would have children and care for them and for each other and for the world given them.

Big Raven flew back into space where he lives. But he still flies down over the earth to see how his creation is being cared for.

A place to have children

Before there was an earth, the spirits of people and animals lived in the lowest part of the heavens. It was a cold, dark place.

"We want to have children and a place where they can grow and be happy," the spirits said. "We have no souls or bodies. We will ask the help of the heavenly beings."

In their search, these spirits traveled to the higher heaven. There they found souls. For a long time, the people and the animals lived together among the stars. But they knew that this was not the end of their search.

Again they set out across the heavens. They sought the advice of the morning and evening stars. "Help us. We have souls. Now we need bodies so that we may have children."

The stars held council. They advised the people. "We cannot give you bodies, but we can guide you through the skies to one who is mightier and wiser. And when you find the bodies you need and the better place to live, we can guide you through the night."

The people continued on and came upon Grandmother Moon. "Help us, Grandmother, we want bodies so that we may have children. We have souls. We have yet to find bodies."

Grandmother Moon said: "I will brighten your nights and divide your days. I will make the waters rise and fall to mark off the passage of time. But I cannot give you bodies. There is one mightier and wiser than I. He alone can give you the bodies you need."

The people continued in their search. In the highest part of the sky, they found Grandfather Sun, the mightiest and wisest of heavenly beings. As the people stood in his dazzling light, they knew he was the one they sought.

Grandfather Sun shone upon them. "I will not only give you bodies so that you may have children. First, I will give you the earth. She will be your Mother so that you and your children will have all you need."

But messengers sent ahead returned with bad news. "There is no land for us to live on. The earth is covered everywhere with water."

The people looked over the animals and decided that Elk was the strongest swimmer. He was chosen to search the earth for land. Elk swam on top of the water and searched beneath it but he could find no land. As he grew tired and felt himself sinking, he gave one last mighty cry. "Help me, Great Winds of the four directions."

The winds came together in a giant crash, causing the waters to rise up into the air. Elk felt solid rock beneath his feet and all around him land appeared above the water. Elk was so overjoyed, he lay down and rolled over and over. Elk's hair soaked up the mud and transformed it into trees and grasses. Soon animals and birds appeared.

The earth was now ready for the people. But how could the people reach it? They called to Red Eagle for help. He turned them into eagles like himself so they could fly down. As they arrived they turned into people with bodies so they could have children on an earth that provided for all their needs.

Creation

High in the heavens, there is a world similar to this world. In this heavenly world, there is a tree known as the "Tree of Life." Long ago, a man was given the job of caring for this sacred tree. He was told he must never allow anyone or anything to disturb it. The man's wife became pregnant and developed a strange craving. "Husband, go and dig at the roots of the tree. There grows the only food that will stop this craving."

The man refused. "No, wife," he said, "the tree is sacred. It must not be disturbed."

His wife became very angry and yelled at the man. Still he would not disturb the tree. The woman's craving grew stronger. If her anger could not make her husband dig at the roots, she would try something else. She began to cry. The man hated to see his wife so unhappy.

"Come, wife, we will dig at the roots. We will find what you need."

With a digging stick, the man dug a hole around the roots of the Tree of Life. The wife could not wait. Getting down on her knees, she leaned over the dark hole to grab the food she craved. Reaching into the darkness, she lost her balance and fell through the hole. She fell in darkness for a very long time. Then she heard whooshing sounds. Many large birds appeared. They caught her on their wings and carried her farther down to where all was water.

A giant turtle rose from the water. "Place her on my back," said the turtle.

"I do not like it here," said the woman. "In my world, there was earth."

Beaver, Otter and Muskrat dove into the water and Muskrat returned with a tiny piece of earth. He placed it on the turtle's back. It began to grow.

Sky Woman was pleased and walked about, watching the earth form. She lay down to sleep and awoke to find a fire and a garden of corn, beans and squash. They became known as the "Three Sister Providers." She gave birth to a girl, whom she named "Gust of Wind."

Gust of Wind was a good daughter who grew into a beautiful young woman. Sky Woman loved her very much. One day, Gust of Wind was picking berries in the woods when she suddenly became tired. She lay down on the soft grass and soon fell into a deep sleep. While she slept, Dream Spirit came to her and waved two arrows over her. One was tipped with cold, hard flint, and the other was made from the wood of a young maple tree. When Gust of Wind woke up, she hurried home to tell her mother her dream.

Sky Woman knew what it meant. "My daughter, you will soon be a mother. You will have twins, two boys. They will be strong and healthy."

Gust of Wind was happy, but not for long. As the twins grew inside her, they fought and argued continuously. They even argued about how to be born. "I will leave my mother through her side," said Flint.

"We must leave our mother the proper way or we will kill her," replied Young Tree.

Flint did not listen to his brother and pushed through his mother's side, killing her. Young Tree could only follow.

Sky Woman was very sad over the death of her daughter. She buried Gust of Wind in the earth she lay on. "My daughter, you have given your life for the life of others. I will raise these boys to love and respect you. They shall know you as Mother Earth."

As the boys grew, they continued to fight and argue. Sky Woman favored Flint, thinking it was Young Tree that killed her beloved daughter. Young Tree knew why his grandmother always sided with Flint but he loved her anyway. He always tried to be kind and helpful. Flint was always mean and disrespectful to his grandmother.

As Sky Woman grew old, the boys continued to fight. When she died, the boys even argued over what to do with her. "Kick her off the edge of the world," said Flint.

"No, we must return her to the daughter she loved so much. We must bury her in the earth," said Young Tree.

As Young Tree picked up his grandmother to place her in the earth, Flint grabbed her head. The head came off and flew up into the dark sky. Young Tree saw his grandmother high above the earth. "Forgive us, Grandmother, and guide us through the darkness. You will be known as Grandmother Moon."

Young Tree liked to create beautiful things. But all he created Flint would find a way to destroy or rearrange. When Young Tree created roses, Flint added thorns. Young Tree created

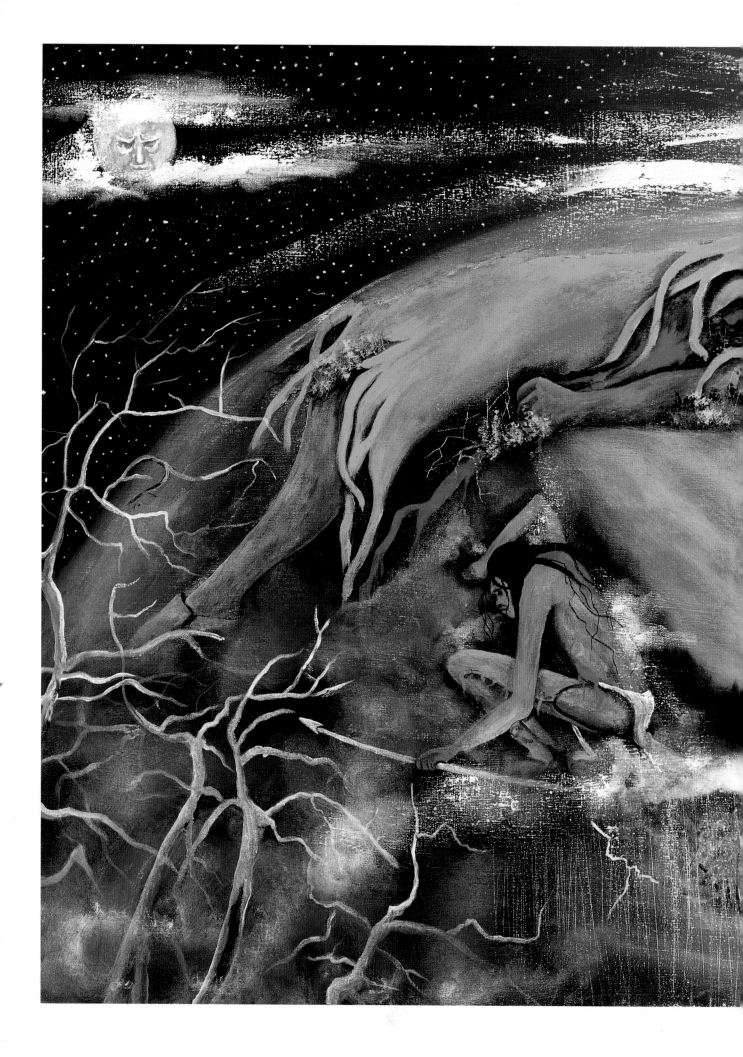

rivers to flow in two directions to ease traveling. Flint made the rivers flow in only one direction, and threw large rocks into the waters to make traveling even more difficult.
One day, after Young Tree had created all the animals, he noticed the woods were very quiet. No birds sang. No animals could be seen. "Brother, what have you done? Where are my animals? Where are my birds?"

"I have hidden them away," Flint answered. "I plan on changing them."

"I will fight you," Young Tree challenged. "Whoever wins shall rule the world. Whoever loses shall live in darkness."

Flint agreed to the fight. He made himself a spear from a branch and a stone. Young Tree used the antler of a deer. They fought for a long time. Flint was winning, but as he ran to spear his brother, he slipped and fell on Young Tree's antler. Flint lost the fight. He begged his brother not to kill him. Young Tree took pity on Flint. "Go and live in darkness," he said, and banished Flint to the underworld.

Young Tree then went on to create mountains and lakes and trees and flowers. Then he came upon a stranger, a man. "What are you doing here?" asked Young Tree. "The earth is not quite ready for humans."

"This is my world, not yours," the stranger said. "I created it and I will rule it."

"You think you are the creator? We will have a test. Whoever can make the mountains move shall rule the world. The loser shall serve mankind."

The stranger spoke in a loud voice. "Mountains, I command you to move." Nothing happened.

Young Tree spoke. "Move, Mountains!"

There was a loud noise. The mountain came so fast and hard the stranger didn't have time to move. The mountain hit him in the face, twisting it out of shape. Young Tree had won the contest.

"I have lost," said the stranger. "How shall I serve mankind?"

"Go into the woods," Young Tree ordered. "Carve your image into the trees. With these images, you will serve mankind by curing sickness. You will be known as 'False Face.' You will give the people medicine."

At last, the earth was ready for man. Young Tree went to the water's edge, took some red clay and molded it into the shape of a human being. "I will give you a portion of my sight. I will give you a portion of my mind and a portion of my blood. With my breath, you shall have life."

Young Tree held man in his hand and presented him to the earth. "This is the earth, our mother. All you will need is here. Love and respect her, and she will always provide."

Young Tree gave Mother Earth to the people to care for. He then returned to the home of his grandmother in the heavens, from where he could look down on his creation.

Bones in the basket

There was a time when there was only Creator and his daughter in the world. Creator decided his world needed people. He heard of a place called "the Land of the Spirits" where there were people.

That land was far underground and difficult to reach. Many steep and dangerous cliffs had to be climbed down on the long journey. After days of exhausting travel, Creator and his daughter arrived in the Land of the Spirits.

It was a strange place where little light entered, even in the daytime. The spirits who lived there were even stranger. They became people only at night. Every evening, as soon as all light disappeared, they came out of their lodges to dance and sing. Then, at the first light of dawn they returned to their lodges, lay down and turned into dry bones.

Creator planned how he might capture these spirits and take them back to people his world. He asked his daughter to weave a basket. That night he watched until dawn came and the spirits hurried home and lay down. As soon as they turned into dry bones, he and his daughter gathered the bones into the basket.

With the basket strapped to his back, Creator climbed up the steep path to his home. As he neared the top, he slipped and the basket fell. The bones spilled out and ran scared back down the path to the dark world below. His daughter who was following behind tried to stop them, but they were too fast for her.

Creator and his daughter went back to the Land of the Spirits and again gathered the bones. And a second time, as

Creator reached the top of the path, he dropped the basket. The bones again ran back to their lodges. The third time Creator and his daughter almost reached their home before the basket fell.

This time Creator tried to reason with the bones. "Why are you frightened?" he asked. "Why do you want to run back to the world below and come alive only in the dark? In my world you will see the day is more beautiful than the night. You won't want to sleep it away. There is sunshine, a big sky, great mountains and so much to see."

The bones seemed to understand. They stopped running and lay down so that Creator and his daughter could put them back into the basket.

When Creator and his daughter arrived back in their world, the sun was rising. They sat among the beautiful mountains as the morning mist melted. Creator reached into the basket. In his hand he held, not bones, but people. They looked around at the world he had brought them to and liked what they saw. As Creator pulled out the people, he threw each handful toward the four directions.

He called out the names of animals and fish, and as he spoke each name, that creature appeared on earth to provide for the new people.

Creator and his daughter then left the world they had created and built a lodge where the sun rises and where they could look down on their creation.

The tribes

The **CHUCKCHEE** (also Chukchi) live in the easternmost part of Russian Siberia, across the Bering Strait from Alaska. They are a part of the family of groups that include Eskimos and Inuits and whose territory extends from northern Siberia to Greenland, including most of Alaska and all of northern Canada.

The **CREE** live in an area that extends from the woodlands of northern Quebec to the plains of Alberta, the largest geographic distribution of any tribe in Canada. Traveling by canoe during summers and snowshoes and toboggans in the winter, they hunted moose, caribou, geese, ducks and fish. Today the Cree family continues to live in a large area from James Bay, Quebec, in the east, to northern Alberta in the west.

The **MANDAN** originally inhabited an area that is now Ohio but migrated to an area on the Missouri River in present day South Dakota before their first contact with white explorers in 1738. In 1837, the tribe was almost wiped out by a smallpox epidemic and the population continues to be small as a result. They traveled and traded extensively with Europeans in the upper Missouri region and gained a reputation as a helpful and friendly people. They continue to live in South Dakota.

The **MODOC** lived in northern California and southern Oregon. They came into contact with Europeans relatively recently and are perhaps most famous for the Modoc War of 1872-73. After the war, part of the tribe was sent to live in Oklahoma. The rest continue to live in Oregon and northern California. Related to other tribes in the Pacific Northwest, the Modoc used canoes to fish for food and were known for their basket weaving.

The **MOHAWK**, the easternmost member of the Iroquois Confederacy, lived in northeastern New York. In colonial times, they often battled the French with the support of the British. After American independence, they settled in southern Ontario and Quebec, where they live today.

The **OSAGE** occupied a territory that included most of Missouri and parts of Arkansas and Kansas. They made war with neighboring tribes so often that in many of these tribes the word for enemy became *osage*. In 1808, they signed a treaty ceding most of their land to the United States and they were moved to northeastern Oklahoma where they live today.

The **ZUÑI** are said to descend from two distinct peoples, one of whom came from the north, to be joined later by a group from the west. In 1539, Spanish explorers from Mexico saw evidence of Zuñi settlements and described their territory as the "Kingdom of Cibola." The Spanish set up many missions and settlements on Zuñi land, all of which failed until the arrival of the Americans. The Zuñi now live on two reserves, one in western New Mexico and the other in northeastern Arizona.